Goodbye, Tommy

Adèle Geras has written more than eighty books for children and young adults, including *Troy* and the *Little Swan* series. She enjoys writing ghost stories and this book was inspired by the house that she's lived in for twenty years. She and her husband have two grown-up daughters and she loves reading, going to the movies and the theatre. She spends lots of good writing time emailing her friends. Her first novel for adults has recently been published.

www.adelegeras.com

Shock Shop is a superb collection of short, illustrated, scary books for younger readers by some of today's most acclaimed writers for children.

Other titles in Shock Shop:

Stealaway K. M. Peyton
The Bodigulpa Jenny Nimmo
Long Lost Jan Mark
Hairy Bill Susan Price
You Have Ghost Mail Terence Blacker
The Beast of Crowsfoot Cottage Jeanne Willis
Wicked Chickens Vivian French

SHOCK SHOP

Goodbye, Tommy Blue

Adèle Geras

Illustrated by David Wyatt

MACMILLAN CHILDREN'S BOOKS

First published 2003 by Macmillan Children's Books

This edition published 2003 by Macmillan Children's Books
a division of Macmillan Publishers Limited
20 New Wharf Road, London N1 9RR
Basingstoke and Oxford
www.panmacmillan.com

Associated companies throughout the world

ISBN 0 330 41570 0

Text copyright © Adèle Geras 2003
Illustrations copyright © David Wyatt 2003

The right of Adèle Geras and David Wyatt to be identified as the
author and illustrator of this work has been asserted by them in accordance
with the Copyright, Designs and Patents Act 1988.

1 3 5 7 9 8 6 4 2

A CIP catalogue record for this book is available from
the British Library.

Typeset by Intype London Ltd
Printed and bound in Great Britain by Mackays of Chatham plc, Kent

To K. M. Peyton

Contents

Chapter 1
The Ghost   1

Chapter 2
The New Neighbours   13

Chapter 3
The Ghost Comes Back   25

Chapter 4
The Brigade   35

Chapter 5
Telling Rachel   47

Chapter 6
A Hole in the Floor   55

Chapter 7
Telling Luke   69

Chapter 1
The Ghost

Nell saw the ghost on the day that the whole family went to look round 12, Maymoor Crescent for the very first time. Nell's parents were determined to buy the house, because Nell's mum had fallen in love with the stained glass window in the front hall. She sometimes saw its colour glowing, lit from inside as she walked home from the bus stop on winter evenings and couldn't get over how beautiful it was.

"If ever that house comes on the market,"

she used to say, "we'll move."

When the estate agent's board appeared in the front garden, Mrs Miller was the first person to phone and ask to look round. The family moving out were called the Watsons, and they had to leave quickly, because Mr Watson had just been sent abroad by the bank where he worked. This suited the Millers, because when Nell's dad saw the house, he fell in love with it as well. By the time they all went round it together, her parents had already made an offer, the Watsons had left, and Nell hoped very much that she and her elder sister, Rachel, would also like it, because if they didn't it wouldn't have made any difference.

When she noticed that there was someone, or something, in the room with them, the first thing she realized was that no one else could see it. She thought of saying something to Rachel, but then thought better of it. She couldn't say anything while their parents were around, and later, she knew, her elder sister would be plugged into her Walkman, or texting someone on her mobile phone. She'd probably laugh at her, anyway, and her parents would either say that she was letting her imagination run away with her as usual, or else think that she was sickening for something.

So Nell decided to keep quiet. She might not have been able to stop herself from screaming if the ghost had been frightening in any way, but after the cold shock that came over her when she first caught sight of it, she was surprised to find herself feeling curious and amazed and not chilled to the bone with terror, which is what she would have expected.

The ghost was in one of the back bedrooms, standing in a corner. Maybe, Nell thought, he's not scary because he's only a boy, and he looks even younger than I am. She was nine and this boy was shorter than she was. She wondered at first whether Mum and Dad and Rachel could see him as well, but when her mother walked right into him, talking about something completely different, she realized that she was the only one in the family who knew he was there. If Rachel had got even a glimpse of the way he was dressed, she would have shrieked. His clothes weren't the least bit trendy. He was wearing long shorts, a white shirt and a sleeveless pullover. He was grey all over, and Nell didn't know whether his clothes really were that colour or if he looked like that because you could see through him to the whiteish wall beyond.

Mum had already decided that this was Nell's bedroom. She looked out of the window and spoke over her shoulder:

"We thought this room for you, Nell. What d'you think? Rachel, you'll like the one at the end of the corridor. Go and have a look. It's more private."

Rachel went off at once.

"It's lovely and big, Nell, isn't it?" Mum continued. "And you've got a good view of next door's garden, which is far nicer than ours. I'll have to get cracking after we move in."

Mum and Dad disappeared then to examine the bathroom, and for a moment Nell wondered whether she ought to follow her parents. Did she really want to be all alone with a ghost? She glanced over to where he was standing. He was thin and dark and looked a little like a picture projected on to the wall. As she watched, he moved away from the corner and sat on the floor and put his head between his hands. He looked so sad that Nell knew she had to speak.

"Hello," she said. "I wonder what your name is." She felt stupid whispering, but she had to. She didn't want her parents coming back to see why she was talking to herself. For a split second she thought that the ghost looked straight at her, but then he got up and went to the window and she couldn't see his face any more. She felt disappointed and it occurred to her that he might have been as astonished to see her as she was to see him.

This might have been his bedroom long ago, she thought. I'll have to ask Mum about who used to live here before the Watsons. She crossed the room and the shadowy figure

began to dissolve. He'd disappeared completely by the time she reached the window, and Nell looked all round for him. Next door's garden *was* lovely, just as her mother had said: a velvety square of smooth lawn surrounded by neat flowerbeds full of leafy shrubs and rose bushes which had very few roses on them because it was almost October.

An old lady came round the corner of the house from the front. She walked slowly, as though every step was an effort.

"Seen everything, Nell?" Nell's mother put her head round the door.

"Look, Mum, it's the old lady from next door."

"Mrs Sparrow," said Mum. "That's her name. Marjorie Sparrow. She's a widow, and she must really rattle around in a house this size. But I suppose she's attached to it.

Her husband only died last year. Imagine! He spent his whole life in these two houses. This one and the one next door."

"This one? What d'you mean?" Nell asked.

"Well, it's what's called a semi-detached house. Two houses joined together by a common wall. This one was built in 1911, and Mr Sparrow was born in our part of the house. When he met Marjorie, and they wanted to get married, the other half of the semi happened to be up for sale, so they bought it. Then after

Mr Sparrow's parents died, this part of the house was sold, but Marjorie and her husband went on living next door. Now of course, it's her on her own."

"How come you know this?" Dad asked. He'd come back while Mum had been speaking.

"I went and introduced myself when I first came to look round," Mum answered. "It's very important to get to know your neighbours. She's very nice, Mrs Sparrow, though I do feel sorry for her, now she's all alone. She's got a daughter and a grandson, but it must be lonely most of the time."

"I wish there were children next door," Nell said.

"Can't have everything," said Mum. "I expect the grandson might come and visit from time to time. Go and find Rachel, Nell, and we'll go home. There's lots to be done if we want to move in quickly."

Nell looked round the room once more before she left, in case the ghost had returned, but she couldn't see him anywhere.

"Goodbye," she whispered as she closed the door behind her. "I hope you're here when I come back."

She thought about the little boy all the way home and wondered why he'd seemed so sad. No, Nell decided, he wasn't really sad. More anxious. That was it. She wondered whether she would ever find out what was worrying him.

Chapter 2
The New Neighbours

Luke Whitley was hanging around the front garden of his grandmother's house, hoping to get a look at the family moving in next door. Gran had told him that one of the children was a girl of about his age. Luke loved coming to visit his grandmother, but it would be even more fun from now on if there was someone next door to play with, even if that someone wasn't a boy.

The furniture van had been and he'd watched removal men carrying beds and

chairs and tables and
chests of drawers into number
12. The Millers were already in the house.
He'd only got a glimpse of them as they
went in and he'd tried to peer in at the
window of the front room but there was
nobody there. He decided to go round and
see if he could spot them from the back.

The girl, the one Gran had told him about, was actually in the garden. She obviously wasn't expecting anyone to appear suddenly, because she gasped when she saw him and put her hand over her mouth. Luke said quickly, "You've just moved in next door, haven't you?"

He went over and stood by the hedge and smiled at her. She was wearing red tracksuit bottoms with a fleece top.

"Yes," she said. "But who are you?"

"I'm Luke Whitley. My gran lives here. We're visiting. We come here quite a lot really. What's your name?"

"Nell," said the girl. "Nell Miller. Well, it's Eleanor really, but everyone calls me Nell. That's my window up there. I can see right into your gran's garden. It's really great. Ours is a bit of a mess, but Mum says we'll tidy it up before the summer. It's a bit cold now."

"Why've you come out, then?"

"Because everything's a mess inside. Whenever I sit down somewhere, my mum comes and moves me away because she wants to arrange something, or decorate something or . . . I don't know. It's going to be ages till everything's straight. It's awful. We can't even put the carpets down because tomorrow the rewiring starts. Men are

coming to fix all kinds of electrical things and Dad says they'll be tearing up the floorboards and everything."

"You can come and play with me, if you like. I'll ask Gran but I'm sure she won't mind. She'll be pleased, I expect. She's always asking me if I'm missing my friends."

"That'd be great," said Nell. "I'd love to see what the other half of the house is like. My sister says I'm nosy, but I'm not really. I just like seeing how other people live, that's all. And you can come and visit me when my room is sorted out."

"Right," said Luke. "I'm going in now. Ask your mum and I'll ask Gran. See if you can come at teatime. Gran makes good cakes."

"OK. Thanks. I'd better go in now. My mum will want me to help even though there's nothing much I can do. I can't even unpack my things properly. See you later."

Luke watched her going up the steps to her back door, and he went indoors to let Gran know that he'd met one of the new neighbours and she was quite nice. Not as good as a boy would have been, but OK.

"Come in, come in, my dear," said Marjorie Sparrow. "Luke tells me you're hiding away from all the disturbance. Moving in *is* a lot of hard work, isn't it? Luke, take Nell into the kitchen and give her a slice of the chocolate cake."

"Come on," said Luke, and he set off down the corridor.

"It's just like our house," said Nell, "but the other way round. And it's very . . . I don't know the right word."

"Old-fashioned," Luke whispered.

"That's what I think as well. But I like it. It's not a bit like my house."

"Nor like our old house," said Nell. "I don't know what the new house is going to look like by the time it's all tidy again."

Luke could feel Nell looking at him as he cut the cake and put it carefully on two plates.

"Why are you staring at me like that?"

"Was I?" Nell blushed. "I'm sorry.

It's just that you look . . . you look a bit like someone I know."

"Who do I look like?"

"Doesn't matter," said Nell. "This is ace cake. Did your gran make it?"

Luke couldn't answer because his mouth was full, so he just nodded. As soon as he'd finished his cake, he said, "Come into the lounge and I'll show you something."

They went into the front room. There were dark green velvet curtains at the window and a glass-fronted cupboard stood against the far wall. Luke opened the doors very carefully and took out a wooden box.

"Let's sit on the sofa," he said. "It's easier to look at them when you're sitting down."

"Are we allowed to sit on it?" Nell wanted to know. It was a very large sofa, upholstered in dark velvet, and didn't look very comfortable. There were no squashy

20

cushions to sink into.

"Why not?" Luke looked puzzled.

"Well, it's very . . . very posh."

"No, it isn't," said Luke. "It's just that no one sits on it much so it doesn't get worn out, that's all. It's OK, really." He opened the box and took out a bag made of velvet, which looked a little like the bag Nell used to carry her gym shoes to school. "What d'you think of these?"

Luke opened the bag, and tipped some small figures on to the sofa. Nell bent her head to have a better look.

"Toy soldiers!" she said. "Ace! They look dead old. Are they yours?"

There must have been about twenty of them. They weren't very big; about the size of her *Star Wars* figurines. Each one wore a blue uniform trimmed with gold. They all had painted blue eyes and red mouths, and wore tall, black military caps.

"They're quite old, I suppose. And yes, they're mine."

"They're lovely," said Nell. "You're really lucky."

"I know," said Luke. "My grandad left them to me when he died. But I keep them here to play with when I come and visit my gran. She likes them too, you see. They remind her of Grandad."

"What sort of games do you play with them?" Nell wanted to know.

"All sorts. Come on, let's take them upstairs and I'll show you."

Chapter 3
The Ghost Comes Back

Nell couldn't get to sleep. The bed was her bed from the old house, and the duvet was the one she tucked around her every night, but the room felt strange and chilly. All her toys and her clothes were still in boxes, stacked up between the chest of drawers and the wall. The uncarpeted floor stretched out from her bed to the door, and she could see the small triangle of light shining in on to the bare planks from the light that was always left on all night. Some people, Nell

thought, would
have said she
was babyish to
need a night-
light, but she
didn't care what
anyone thought as
long as she didn't
have to see the dark-
ness being dark and
scary if she happened to
wake up before daybreak.
She was being extra-
babyish now, and
cuddling Dodger, the fat
yellow teddy bear who
normally just sat on her
pillow. In the old house, she
used to push him down to the end of the bed
when she got into it. Sometimes she had to

pick him up from the floor in the morning because she'd kicked him off the bed during the night without knowing it. Here, though, in her new room, she needed Dodger to keep her company. She hadn't forgotten that this room also belonged to a ghost, even though she hadn't seen him yet this evening.

She lay in the half-dark and closed her eyes. I'll think about Luke, she said to herself. She'd nearly told him that he reminded her of a ghost, but she'd stopped herself just in time. Luke's gran was nice, and they'd had a good game with his soldiers, up in Luke's bedroom. Nell hadn't played soldiers before, but it turned out to be just like playing with dolls.

"Only we had to keep marching up and down," she whispered to Dodger. "And then we had to lie them all down in two rows in a castle made out of cardboard. A bit like a dolls' house, really, but not as nice."

She thought longingly of her own dolls' house, which hadn't even been brought upstairs yet. She wondered whether there would be carpet left over from the one she'd helped choose for this room, which Mum would allow her to cut up for the dolls' rooms. Suddenly, she heard someone whispering in her ear.

"Tommy Blue," the voice was saying. "Where are you?"

Nell sat straight up in bed and looked around her, shivering. Who was it, whispering like that? It was such a sad sound. Could she have dreamed it? Or was it . . . could it be . . . the ghost?

"Is it you? Little boy? Have you come back again? Please tell me what's wrong!"

She peered into the darkest corner of the room, where the packing cases full of her things made a sort of mountain range against the wall. As she stared, she saw the boy's outline being filled in gradually. It was just as though someone was colouring in a drawing. After a few seconds, he was there, looking like a real person, only not as solid. One of the boxes *had* been opened. It was the one that her duvet and her bed-toys, like Dodger, had been packed in. The ghost was actually searching in it, putting his hand right into it and moving things around.

"Hey!" said Nell, jumping out of bed. "You can't go looking in my stuff like that. I don't care if you *are* a ghost. I don't care if this *is* your old room. I live here now and it's rude to rummage about in other people's things."

"Tommy Blue!" said the ghost, moving away from the box and drifting to the

window where the old curtains, the Watson family's curtains, were tightly closed and keeping out the night.

"There's no one called Tommy Blue here. I'm Nell. What's your name?"

"Tommy Blue . . ." said the ghost. Nell sighed. Maybe that *was* his name.

"Was this your room once?" she asked, hoping that if she changed the subject, the

ghost might say something a bit more interesting.

"Where are you?" said the ghost but, as he spoke, Nell could see that his outline was becoming misty. He was fading, disappearing. As she watched, he vanished altogether and she was alone again, and didn't feel a bit sleepy.

"But I'd better try, hadn't I, Dodger?" she

said to her teddy bear. She picked him up from the floor. He'd fallen on to the bare boards when she'd leaped out of bed. She hugged him tight and said, "I hope you haven't got splinters in your bum! Mum says we have to watch out for splinters."

She lay back against the pillows and wondered whether she ought to tell someone about her ghost. Her parents were busy getting the house ready, and worrying about the rewiring and whether the carpets would be delivered on time, and wondering if the new curtains would look as good as they did in the shop. They wouldn't pay proper attention. Perhaps she could say something to Luke, but she didn't really know him well enough to tell if he'd laugh at her or not.

She thought about the ghost in his old-fashioned pullover and short trousers. Then she thought about Luke in his trainers (with a silver flash on the sides) and his baseball cap (which he liked so much that he hadn't even taken it off when they were indoors) and she realized that Luke didn't just look a little bit like the ghost. He could have been the ghost's twin brother. She went on wondering about how that could possibly be until at last she fell asleep with Dodger clutched tightly in her arms.

Chapter 4
The Brigade

Nell was sitting at the kitchen table in Mrs Sparrow's house, with Luke opposite her and Mrs Sparrow in the chair next to hers. Rachel had gone round to visit a friend of hers who lived nearby, and Nell had been invited next door.

"To give your mother some space," said Mrs Sparrow. "And things will go much more quickly if she doesn't have to worry about feeding you, won't they?"

"Yes, I suppose they will," said Nell, who

didn't know whether to feel pleased at being asked next door for lunch or offended because Mrs Sparrow and her mother thought she might have been a nuisance during the unpacking and rewiring, which she certainly wouldn't. When she saw the cottage pie that Mrs Sparrow put on the table, with the mashed potato on top baked into wavy stripes of golden brown, she made up her mind to enjoy herself.

Luke was talking about his soldiers. Nell was too busy at first, looking around at the plates and jugs on Mrs Sparrow's dresser and then eating the pie which was just as delicious as it looked, to take much notice of what he was saying, but then she heard him ask his grandmother a question.

"My Brigade," he said. "Are they wearing the same uniform that Grandpa wore when he was a soldier?"

"Goodness me, no," said Mrs Sparrow. "Your grandfather was in the army during the Second World War. The Brigade was old-fashioned even when he was a boy."

She finished eating, put her knife and fork tidily on her plate, and patted her mouth with a paper napkin.

"Edwin was a little boy during the First World War. His father – that's your great-grandfather, Luke – fought during that war.

1914 to 1918 . . . a very long time ago. But the Brigade was a present to him on his fifth birthday, and the soldiers are all wearing what they might have worn during the Crimean War, which was fought during the 1850s. Florence Nightingale nursed the wounded during that war. Have you learned about her at school? They called her the Lady with the Lamp. But the tall hats with braid on them, and the jackets with lovely gold buttons on the front, was what the uniform looked like in those days."

"Grandad loved the Brigade, didn't he?"

"He certainly did." She smiled at Nell and

explained: "My husband used to take the soldiers out and, well, not exactly play with them. He was a little old for that, of course, but he *did* set them out in rows and look at them and he always put them back in their bag. He loved it when Luke came to stay and they could play a proper game."

She laughed. "He couldn't fool me though. He always said that the game was played for Luke's sake, but just between you and me, Nell, I think he enjoyed those times just as much as Luke did. Maybe even more."

"I know," said Nell. "My dad likes playing computer games. He says he's only joining in with us, but he's the one who never wants to stop."

Luke and his grandmother laughed. Then Mrs Sparrow said, "There's bananas and grapes for afters, children. Help yourselves."

She turned to Nell. "It's the rewiring today, isn't it?"

Nell nodded. "When I came over, they'd just started on my room. They won't finish today, either. Mum says I'll have to be extra careful. I've been having to walk very slowly so as not to get splinters in my feet from the floorboards, and now there'll be holes in the floor as well."

"Can we go and play now, Gran?" Luke asked.

"Yes, of course, but just before you do, there's something I want to show you both. Luke, you've seen it before, of course, but I'm sure Nell would be interested."

"Is it the photograph?" Luke sounded a little embarrassed.

"Yes, it is," said Mrs Sparrow. "What's wrong with that?"

"Nothing," said Luke. "I suppose."

They all got up from the table and went into the front room.

"I'm going to get the soldiers out," said Luke. "I've seen those photos before a million times."

"Don't mind him, Nell dear," said Mrs Sparrow. "Go and sit on the sofa and I'll fetch the album."

Nell sat down and waited. Mrs Sparrow did everything rather slowly, but there was a lot to look at. Soon, she was sitting down next to Nell on the posh sofa.

"This is Edwin's album," she said, opening up a thick, leather-bound volume. "I've got one too, full of pictures of me as a girl, but I wanted you to see something in particular."

She began to turn the pages quite quickly and Nell caught glimpses of men and ladies in dark clothes and hats, and then there was a baby on a furry rug. There he was again, a little older this time, on his mother's lap, and then she saw a toddler with rather long, curly dark hair, wearing knickerbockers and a funny sort of shirt with a lacy collar.

"We can go back and look at Edwin as a baby if you like but this was the one I wanted you to see."

She pointed a finger at a photograph of a boy. He looked about nine years old and he was standing next to a tree, holding the hand of a lady dressed in a lacy blouse and a long dark skirt.

"That's the pear tree in your back garden, dear," said Mrs Sparrow. "Do you recognize it?"

"Oh, yes," said Nell. "But I didn't know it was a pear tree. Is that Luke's grandfather?"

"That's right. And his mother, my mother-in-law. Her name was Sylvia. She was very

beautiful, don't you think? But look at
Edwin. Who does he remind you of?"

Nell knew what Mrs
Sparrow wanted her
to say and so she
said it: "He looks
just like Luke,
doesn't he?"

"That's right. Luke gets tired of me pointing it out to everyone, but it comforts me to think that there's a part of Edwin I can still see."

Nell nodded, and stared at the photograph. She felt a sudden chill come over her. No, she wasn't mistaken. It was true. The boy in the photograph *was* her ghost: the one who appeared and disappeared in her room. She was as certain about it as she'd ever been about anything. Her house was haunted by the young Edwin Sparrow, which made sense when you thought about it. Their house had been his house when he was a boy. But why did he keep coming back to her room? And why was he so sad? And what had he been looking for among her possessions?

Mrs Sparrow went on turning the pages of the photograph album, but Nell was wondering whether she ought to tell someone else about him. Perhaps she should talk to Mrs Sparrow? Or Luke? Or maybe her parents? Would anyone believe her? She didn't know what to do so she decided to do nothing, just for the moment. She'd think about it later, when she got home.

Chapter 5
Telling Rachel

"Do you believe in ghosts, Rachel?"

"Hmm?" Rachel wasn't really listening. She and Nell had been sent down to the supermarket to do the shopping, because Mum and Dad were so busy at the house. They usually enjoyed this, because Mum always gave them a fiver and they stopped to have a drink in the supermarket café. Today, Rachel had asked for a cappuccino, and Nell knew she'd only ordered it to seem more grown-up. She was eating the foam off the

top with a spoon.
Her Walkman
wasn't plugged
in, but still, her
attention kept
wandering.

"I said, do you
believe in ghosts?"

"Dunno. I've
never seen one."

"I have," said
Nell, and then she
added, just because Rachel was still not
paying proper attention, "There's one in
my room."

"What? You're kidding me . . ."

"No, I'm not. I saw him the very first time
we looked round the house."

"Why didn't you say anything?"

"You'd have laughed. Mum and Dad

would probably have sent me to the doctor's."

"I think I'm going to laugh now. You're obviously imagining it."

"No, I'm not. I know who he is as well."

That silenced Rachel. She looked, Nell thought, rather pale. As though she'd seen a ghost. That thought made her giggle.

"What are you giggling about?" said Rachel. "If it's true then it's quite serious. We must tell someone."

"I don't see why. He's not doing any harm."

Rachel leaned towards Nell and said, rather breathlessly, "Who is he? What does he do? When you see him, I mean."

Nell smiled. It wasn't often that Rachel listened so carefully to what she said. "Nothing much. He just sort of drifts about."

"What does he look like?" She shivered.

"Like a little boy. Because that's what he is. He looks about nine, like me."

Rachel snorted. "I thought you meant a proper ghost."

"What d'you mean, proper?"

"You know. Spooky. All floaty white bits. Maybe bones showing through, or dragging chains. Or perhaps bloodstained hands or something."

Nell shook her head. "Sorry. No blood-stains."

Rachel was starting to look bored. She began to fiddle with the earpieces on her Walkman. Nell said quickly, "But he does talk."

"What's he say, then?"

"He says, 'Tommy Blue. Where are you?'"

"Bo-ring!" said Rachel.

"It's not boring," Nell said. "I know who he is."

"You WHAT? Who is he, then?"

"He's the ghost of Mr Sparrow. You know, the husband of Mrs Sparrow who lives next door. When he was young, I mean."

"You can't know that's who it is. Not possibly."

"Yes I can, so there! Mrs Sparrow showed us an album and there was a photograph in it of her husband when he was a little boy. I recognized him at once."

"I don't believe it," said Rachel. "I don't believe any of it. You saw the photo first and *then* imagined you saw the ghost. I bet that's how it was and you're just mixing it up."

"I AM NOT!" Nell shouted.

"Sssh!" said Rachel. "Don't be so stupid. You're making a show of yourself."

Nell picked up her glass and drank the rest of her Coke in one gulp. Rachel was the stupid one. She wished now that she'd never mentioned the ghost, and she wondered whether she ought to tell Luke about it. "You're not to say anything to Mum and Dad, Rachel. Promise?"

"Course I won't. I don't need them interrogating me about what's wrong with you." She pushed the earpieces of the Walkman into her ears and pressed the button marked 'Play'. Nell sighed. Rachel wasn't going to be any help at all. She hadn't even got round to telling her about how desperately he'd been looking for something. She wondered, as she'd wondered a thousand times since she first caught sight of him, what exactly he was searching for.

Chapter 6
A Hole in the Floor

"I'm putting a camp bed into Rachel's room for you," said Mum. "You can't possibly sleep in your room while half the floorboards are up."

Nell took a forkful of mashed potato and ate it before she spoke. She knew that it was probably no use making a fuss. When Mum decided something was going to happen, it generally did, and anyway, Nell quite liked spending the night with Rachel. It meant a much later bedtime, for one thing, because as Rachel said, "You can't expect a twelve year old to go to sleep at the same time as a nine year old so Nell will just have to have a late night."

"I don't mind," Nell was quick to add. "I don't need much sleep, really."

This suppertime, Mum and Dad were busy discussing the garden, and when they were ever going to get a chance to drive to the plant nursery together. Nell looked at Rachel, and wondered why she hadn't moaned about having to share her room. She leaned over to whisper in her sister's ear, "You don't mind, do you, Rachel? It'll be fun."

"I'm not thrilled at the idea, if you want to know," Rachel whispered back. "But it'll give you a night or two off from sharing your room with a ghost."

*

Nell was finding it hard to go to sleep on the camp bed. Rachel was already snoring a little. They'd chatted in the dark for a while after Rachel got into bed, and Nell wondered why her sister was so different  when the lights were out. It was almost as though she forgot she had to be much older than Nell, and she seemed quite happy to talk about all sorts of things she would never have mentioned during daylight hours, such as what Chris (a boy she really liked) said to her while they were dancing at the end-of-term disco, and why she was cross with Marie, her best friend, for going to the ice-rink with Sadie and not telling her. Nell had listened and said the odd word just to encourage Rachel and then, at last, silence had fallen and she was left wide awake and looking up at the ceiling.

She heard Mum and Dad getting ready for bed, and soon there wasn't a sound to be heard anywhere in the house. The landing light was on as usual. Far away, a dog was barking. Then, all of a sudden, she heard a noise.

She sat up in the camp bed and listened. What was that? Perhaps it was her ghost, come back to see what was going on in the room that used to be his. But this was more like a tapping, as though it was the house itself that was sending out a signal to her. It's none of my business, she thought, and anyway, perhaps it will stop in a minute. But the noise went on: *tap, tap* and then after a pause, *tap, tap* once more. Nell decided to go and have a look. It wouldn't take a minute, and even if she couldn't stop it, knowing what it was and where it came from would make her feel better.

She got out of the camp bed carefully and tiptoed across to the door, without even bothering to put on her furry, comfortable slippers. Rachel's room still had the carpet in it from when the Watsons lived in the house, so it was easy not to make a lot of noise. There were a couple of squeaky floorboards outside Mum and Dad's room, but she knew which ones they were, and stepped over them. If anyone woke up, she would just say she was on her way to the loo.

Her bedroom looked a mess. Mum said it would be lovely when the rewiring was finished and the new carpet laid, but at the moment the whole floor was nothing but one hole after another. There were a few planks still down, and Nell thought she could probably creep over to her bed, but she felt a little frightened at the gaping darkness of the spaces under the floorboards. And the thought of what might be in there, like spiders and moths and creepy things whose names she didn't know, made her feel shivery all over.

She hesitated before stepping into the room, but she had to. The noise was coming from over by her toy tower, which was what she called the arrangement of wooden boxes where she kept all her things. As she picked her way from one plank to another, she imagined that creatures in the black spaces under the floor were about to put out clammy hands and grab her by the ankles. When she reached her own bed, she jumped on to it and made sure to sit with her legs crossed so that nothing that was hiding underneath could touch the soles of her feet.

She looked around. Everything was so shadowy that she would have welcomed a visit from the ghost. She whispered,

"Ghost? Where are you? You can come if you like."

No one answered her. But the tapping continued. It was definitely coming from . . . she leaned over for a better look, because something had caught her eye: something that glittered. Yes, there it was. The light from the landing was falling on it and making it shine, and Nell knew that if she wanted to stop the tapping, she would have to put her hand into the dark hole in the floor and pick up whatever it was. She took a deep breath. Maybe she ought to call her father and ask him to do it for her. She decided to get a little closer and see if she could see anything.

She got off the bed and knelt close to where the tapping was coming from. Then she leaned right down to the hole and peered into it. What she saw made her catch her breath. It was a toy of some kind: small and covered in dust and cobwebs. Nell didn't know what was making it rock a little backwards and forwards, tapping and tapping, but she did know how to make the noise stop. She took a deep breath, thrust her hand into the hole and closed her fingers round the toy. As quickly as she could, before anything horrible could touch her, she pulled her hand out again and before she'd stopped to think about dirty marks on her

pyjamas, she wiped the toy on her sleeve and had a better look at it.

It was a toy soldier, exactly like all the others in Luke's Brigade. Nell's eyes widened in astonishment. His blue coat was faded. His eyes and mouth had been scratched until you could hardly see them any more, but the painted gold braid on his uniform was still bright.

"That was it: the gold bits on your uniform caught the light," Nell whispered to him. "And they led me to you. You must have been under the floor for years and years and years. Luke's grandfather probably dropped you down there when he was a little boy and you've been there ever since, sort of asleep. I've woken you up, and I'm sorry. Never mind, you can come back to bed with me, and tomorrow I'll take you to Luke's house and you can see all your friends again."

She made her way back to the camp bed in Rachel's room and put the soldier in her slipper. He was too stiff to cuddle, and she didn't want to hide him under her pillow, because he'd just come out of the darkness, and besides, he was still a bit dirty.

"Sleep well," she whispered. She made sure that he couldn't slip down to the toe of her slipper where he wouldn't be able to see the landing light shining in across the floor. Then she lay back and closed her eyes.

She opened them again almost at once and there was the ghost, sitting on the end of the camp bed.

"What are you doing in Rachel's room?" she whispered. "If she wakes up, she'll be terrified."

The ghost smiled and Nell wondered all over again why she wasn't even the least bit afraid of him. She'd grown used to seeing him and now he was looking much happier.

"Thank you," he said.

"What for?"

The ghost didn't answer, but stood up and went to stand next to her slippers.

"Tommy Blue," he sighed, and smiled at her and began to fade away slowly, as though someone were rubbing him out starting at the edges and moving towards the centre.

"Come back!" Nell whispered into the dark. "I think I know who you are now. You're Edwin, aren't you? I know your grandson," she went on. "And your wife. I saw your picture in the album. They miss you so much."

She thought that if the ghost knew all this, he would come back, but he didn't. Perhaps he'd return to her room tomorrow. She lay down again and felt pleased with herself.

"Goodnight, Tommy Blue," she said quietly and hoped that her voice would carry as far as the slipper where she'd put the toy soldier.

Chapter 7
Telling Luke

"Hello, Luke," said Nell. "May I come in? I've got something to show you."

"Yeah," said Luke. "I was going to come round and see if you wanted to play. What've you got?"

"Wait and see. It's a surprise. I've got it wrapped up in my hankie."

Luke's eyes widened. "Is it a dead mouse or something?"

"No, don't be ridiculous. Why would I bring you a dead mouse?"

"I dunno. Because it's interesting?"

"A dead mouse," Nell said "would be *revolting*. This is properly interesting."

"Let's go in the kitchen, then. Gran's just taking some biscuits out of the oven."

Luke led the way and Nell followed.

"Hello, dear," said Mrs Sparrow. "You've come just in time for elevenses."

"I've brought something for Luke," said Nell. "I've been longing to bring it since I woke up, but Mum said I had to wait till everyone had got up and had breakfast and everything. Look. It's a soldier, just like Luke's. Like all the other soldiers from the Brigade."

Luke stared first at the dirty, scratched and faded soldier that Nell had put on the table and then at his grandmother, who had turned very pale. She put the plate with all the biscuits on it down on the table

and sank into one of the chairs.

"Tommy Blue!" she said, and her eyes were suddenly full of tears.

"What's the matter, Gran?" said Luke. "Who's Tommy Blue?"

"That's his name," Nell said. "The soldier's."

Mrs Sparrow turned to stare at Nell. "However do you know that, child? I've never said a word to anyone, I'm sure."

Nell blushed. "Someone else told me," she said.

"But who?" Luke couldn't understand why his grandmother was so bothered about a name. He was just happy to have a member of the Brigade back where he belonged. He said, "I knew there were meant to be twenty-four of them. Twenty-three is a silly sort of number of soldiers to be in a brigade. Kind of uneven. I never said anything, because I just thought Grandpa must have lost one when he was a little boy."

"He did," said Mrs Sparrow. "I never knew about it till he was ill in hospital, just before he died. He was very feverish one day and started talking about someone called Tommy Blue. Babbling, really. I was very upset to see him in that state, I can tell you. Then later, when he was feeling a little better, I asked him about the name, Tommy Blue. That's when he told me that it was one of the soldiers. He lost him. Long ago, when he was not much older than you, Luke, and never found him again. What he said to me was: 'I wish Tommy Blue could be with his regiment. I wish he could.' He kept saying it. I'd always known he was fond of the soldiers, but it wasn't till last year that I understood why they meant so much to him. I told you, didn't I, that his father fought in the First World War?"

Luke and Nell both nodded.

"What I didn't tell you was that he was killed at a battle called the Battle of the Somme. Tommy Blue and the others were all that Edwin had, really, to remind him of his father. That's why he kept them so carefully, and why he was so upset to lose one of their number. I wish he were alive to see this! To see Tommy Blue himself, here on the kitchen table. He'd be so pleased. Thank you for bringing him back, Nell. It was very thoughtful of you."

Luke lined up the soldiers on the desk in the corner of his bedroom: twenty-four of them, in two lines of twelve. He said, "Gran was too upset and excited to notice, but I did."

"Notice what?" Nell asked.

"That you never properly answered her about how you knew Tommy Blue's name. Will you tell me?"

"It doesn't matter. I suppose your gran might have mentioned it."

"No, she never did, Nell. You know that.

There's something you're hiding, isn't there? Come on, you can tell me. I won't let on, I promise."

Nell sighed. "You won't believe me."

"Yes, I will. Go on. Please."

Nell took a deep breath and then started speaking very quickly. "A ghost told me – the ghost of your grandfather when he was a little boy. I recognized him from the photograph in the album, the one of the little boy under the pear tree in our garden. He's been coming into my room for ages, looking for Tommy Blue. I saw him the very first time we came to look round the house. Then last night I found the soldier. Under the floorboards in my bedroom. Because they're rewiring in there. I would never have found him otherwise. That's it."

"*That's it?* You had the ghost of my grandfather in your bedroom and never said anything?" Luke looked hurt and amazed at the same time.

"I didn't think you'd believe me. I thought you'd just laugh."

"I wouldn't have." He frowned. "I just wish I'd seen him, that's all. I've never seen a ghost. And anyway, he was *my* grandfather, not yours."

"I'm sorry," said Nell. "If he ever comes back, I promise I'll phone you and you can come over to have a look."

"Right. OK."

The children sat down on the floor, and Luke began to arrange the soldiers in their cardboard fort. Nell sat and watched him put Tommy Blue in the best place, right near the gate. Then she looked up and cried out before she could help it.

"He's here, Luke. In the corner. The ghost. Look! He's come here!"

Luke turned. He saw a boy, a little like himself, standing in the corner. As the children watched, the ghost drifted over to the fort and knelt down.

"Goodbye, Tommy Blue," he said. Luke's mouth fell open in amazement, and he was trembling. "He can speak," he whispered to Nell.

"Of course he can. I told you he could. That's how I knew the name, remember?"

Luke nodded. "What's happening now, Nell? He's sort of going transparent. He's leaving us, isn't he?"

Nell nodded. "I don't think he'll ever come back, Luke. He's found what he was looking for, and he'll go to wherever it is that ghosts come from, now."

"How do you know?" Luke asked.

"I just do, that's all. He said goodbye. To Tommy Blue, I mean. I think he was saying goodbye to us as well."

Luke picked the little soldier up. "It doesn't matter. I've got Tommy Blue now. I'll look after him." He smiled at Nell. "Thank you for bringing him home."

"That's OK," said Nell. "You're both welcome."

"Both?" Luke looked puzzled.

"You and the ghost. I'm sure he's happy now."

"Me too," said Luke, and then, "OK, come on, it's almost time for a parade."

Nell laughed and helped to line the toy soldiers up on the carpet.

The Beast of Crowsfoot Cottage

Jeanne Willis

A beast is running wild near Crowsfoot Cottage. People keep glimpsing it – huge paw prints, staring eyes, scary shapes at night – but nobody knows what it is. Then terrible things start to happen. Sophie Ellis and her stepdad disappear and the only clues left are drops of blood and some hair.

Frightened rumours begin to fly: it's a werewolf, a great black dog, an animal not of this earth.

What is the truth?

Who will be brave enough to find out . . . ?

Another book in the Shock Shop series . . .

The Bodigulpa

Jenny Nimmo

There's something lurking at the bottom of Daniel's garden. The greenhouse is bursting with peculiar plants and, spookily, grumpy Grandpa Green seems strangely happy. He's always in there talking to the plants while feeding them strange potions.

But something's afoot. First Grandma Green vanishes and then Stanley the dog. Who will be next? Daniel's sure that the greenhouse has something to do with the disappearances. But how can he discover what it is when he's too scared to step inside . . . ?

Another book in the Shock Shop series . . .

Stealaway

K. M. Peyton

Nicky's new home, Bloodybow Castle, is so dark and forbidding. How can Nicky and her mother live in such a spooky place?

But Nicky soon realizes that Bloodybow is haunted by a terrible past. Hundreds of years ago, border raider stole a priceless stallion, starting a feud that led to the death of a young boy.

And now strange events surround Bloodybow once more. A white pony mysteriously comes and goes. Eerie lights are seen at night. And then Stealaway, a beautiful stallion, is threatened. Can Nicky lay a vengeful past to rest – before something terrible happens?

A selected list of titles available from Macmillan Children's Books

The prices shown below are correct at the time of going to press. However, Macmillan Publishers reserve the right to show new retail prices on covers which may differ from those previously advertised.

The Beast of Crowsfoot Cottage	Jeanne Willis	£3.99
The Bodigulpa	Jenny Nimmo	£3.99
Goodbye, Tommy Blue	Adèle Geras	£3.99
Hairy Bill	Susan Price	£3.99
Long Lost	Jan Mark	£3.99
Stealaway	K. M. Peyton	£3.99
Wicked Chickens	Vivian French	£3.99
You Have Ghost Mail	Terence Blacker	£3.99

All Pan Macmillan titles can be ordered from our website, panmacmillan.com, or from your local bookshop and are also available by post from:

Bookpost
PO Box 29, Douglas, Isle of Man IM99 1BQ

Credit cards accepted. For details:
Telephone: 01624 836000
Fax: 01624 670923
E-mail: bookshop@enterprise.net
www.bookpost.co.uk

Free postage and packing in the UK.